IMMORTAL

Written by
Quentin Flynn

Illustrated by
Brent Putze

HORWITZ
MARTIN
EDUCATION

Contents

Chapter **1**

The New Governor Arrives

The fearsome line of soldiers marched, two deep, along the cobblestone street. Their golden armour glinted in the sunlight, and their boots beat out a ferocious sounding rhythm. Deep red plumes fell back from their helmets, and their swords swayed dangerously at their sides, in time to the beat.

"Centurions!" hissed Antonius, pointing at the soldiers. His sister, Marina, looked up from the game of marbles they were playing.

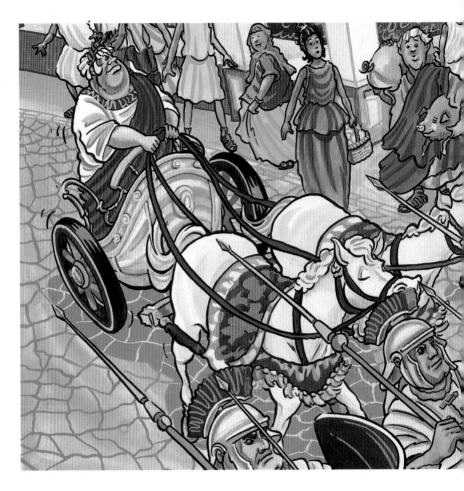

"Who is that?" she whispered, nodding towards
a magnificent golden chariot being drawn by two
fine white horses.

Marina dare not point, in case a guarding centurion
saw her. In the chariot, staring straight ahead, stood
a man draped with a shimmering purple robe.

At the rear of the chariot, a dark purple flag
flapped in the breeze. Antonius squinted his eyes
at the delicate Roman letters, which were woven
on it in gold thread.

"HAIL GRUSIUS!" he read out loud. Antonius
glanced at his sister in excitement.

"It must be Grusius, the new governor of our
town. I heard father talking about him last night.
He said he's a tough man with a brutal reputation.
And he's the emperor's nephew!"

"He doesn't look fearsome," sniffed Marina.
"He just looks like a snob and a bully."

The ground shook as the procession passed by.
The thump of the centurion's boots and the rattle
of the golden chariot bumping over the
cobblestones jarred the earth. Inside the circle
that Marina had drawn with a piece of chalk,
the marbles rolled out of position.

"Whoever he is, he's spoiled our game!"
protested Marina, a little too loudly.

"Shh!" hissed Antonius.

"Do you want to end up on the end of a centurion's sword? No-one dares to insult the new governor!"

Marina looked furious. As the procession wound down the street and out of sight, she picked up the brightly coloured glass marbles, and carefully rearranged them in the circle once more.

"Come on," she said, ignoring her brother's worried look. "I'm sure our snobby governor has better things to do than send his centurions out to arrest children," she added, with a frustrated voice.

And indeed he did.

Reaching the centre of the town, Grusius's chariot came to a halt outside the governor's palace.

Slowly, he looked from side to side, staring at his new home. Glaring at his centurions, he screamed in dismay.

"So *this* is the miserable town of Polonium. What terrible things I must have done to be sent ... here!"

And indeed he had. Grusius had been caught plotting to take power from his uncle, the emperor, and had been lucky to escape with his life. It was only the pleading of the emperor's sister, Grusius's mother, that had saved him.

Instead, the emperor had decided to send his bullying nephew Grusius to the small, faraway town of Polonium. Here, he would be too far from Rome to cause any more problems.

Grusius inspected the square that surrounded his palace. Even though it was a small town, far from the centre of the empire, it still boasted some grand buildings. The governor's palace, of course, was the grandest — with broad steps, seven mighty columns and an arched entrance, decorated with marble carvings and statues.

From where he stood, Grusius could see the fields of grapes and olive trees stretching away into the distance — and on the lower slopes of Mount Pyros.

Like a sleeping giant, Mount Pyros watched over the whole town. In winter, its jagged peak was often hidden by swirling clouds and mist — but on this hot, summery day, it split the blue sky like a steely grey dagger.

"I think I shall rename that mountain 'Mount Grusius'," murmured the governor to himself. "That will remind my lowly townspeople that I will be continually watching over them."

Bored from the lack of attention, he suddenly shouted angrily at his centurions. "Well, am I going to stand here *forever*, or is someone going to help me down?"

Two centurions immediately rushed to the side of their master and helped him out of the chariot. Once safely on the ground, Grusius waved his centurions away in irritation, and strode breathlessly up the steps of his palace.

"Bring in my things. Hurry up!" he shouted, without turning around. "Grusius has important things to do. I'm a very busy man."

Without a word, the centurions did as they were ordered. No-one, not even a well-armed centurion, would dare to question their governor's orders.

Inside, the governor looked around at his palace. The stone walls were covered with murals, and the floor was made up of thousands of tiny tiles, making up a huge circular mosaic. Somewhere in the background, a water fountain bubbled and gurgled. Heavy blue drapes bordered the doorways.

Grusius looked unimpressed. He found a chair, and sat down on it, wiping sweat from his forehead. "Bring me the man called Archius," he ordered loudly.

The centurions looked at each other in terror. Who was Archius? It would mean instant death if they could not find him.

"Somewhere in this tiny excuse for a town lives a man called Archius," shouted the governor. "Find him, and bring him to me. Now!"

Chapter 2

A Task For Archius

Antonius was excitedly telling his father about the arrival of the new governor.

"There were centurions — at least thirty of them — and a pair of white horses, pulling a golden chariot," he recounted breathlessly. "And, in the chariot, was Grusius, the new governor!"

"He looked so smug and snobby in that cart," added Marina sullenly from the corner of the room.

The children's father smiled and looked up from the scroll he was reading. He was surrounded by hundreds of glass jars and earthen pots. Hanging from the ceiling were dozens of bunches of dried herbs and strange plants. This was the 'pharmacia', where the town's people came for their medicines and potions. Archius, the children's father was famous well beyond Polonium for his ability to cure disease and help the sick. His medicines were said to be the best in the country — if not the whole Roman empire.

"You should be careful what you say about our new governor," he said to Marina. "You never know who might be listening."

"Yes, father," said Marina. "But I still say he looks like a big bully!"

Antonius ignored them. "I'm going to be a centurion when I am old enough," he declared.

"I shall wear shiny armour, and march at the head
of the procession. Anyone who even dares to sneeze
when I walk past will feel the tip of my sword!"
Antonius withdrew an imaginary sword from an
imaginary scabbard, and sliced the air wildly.

"I must remember to make up extra batches of anti-sneezing medicine when you are a centurion," chuckled his father. "We mustn't have an outbreak of sneezing while you are marching past."

Suddenly, there was a harsh pounding on the door, and loud shouting coming from the hallway. Antonius forgot all about his imaginary sword, as he heard his mother's protesting voice.

"You can't go in there!" she cried.

Seconds later, three ferocious looking centurions burst into the pharmacia, followed by the children's mother.

"I'm sorry," she said, stretching her hands out to her husband. "I told them you were studying, but they wouldn't listen to me!"

"It's alright, dearest," replied Archius, putting down his scroll and standing up.

Antonius and Marina scurried over to their mother.

"What do you want?" demanded Archius, feeling outraged at the centurions.

"Are you the man they call Archius?" boomed one of the centurions, his hand wavering dangerously over the handle of his sword. The other two centurions looked around the room suspiciously.

"Yes," replied the children's father. "I am Archius."

"You will come with us then," ordered the first centurion. "Grusius, Governor of Polonium, orders you to come now."

Archius smiled at his wife and children, and nodded to the centurion. He gathered his robe around himself, and walked calmly out of the room. The centurions followed, and the house shook as the front door slammed shut.

Marina looked especially terrified.

"It's all my fault," she said, almost crying. "They heard me talking about the governor!"

"Nonsense," replied her mother, giving her a hug. "Governor Grusius probably just has a cold or a sore throat, and needs some medicine."

Antonius was trembling. Face to face, those centurions looked breathtakingly scary. Having seen how mean and brutal they could be, he wasn't so sure that he really wanted to be one any more.

Suddenly, the boy's thoughts were interrupted as the house shook again. But this time, there was no pounding or slamming on the door.

A low, deep growl seemed to be coming from the ground beneath their feet.

Glass jars and earthen pots rattled and bumped into each other as the whole villa shook, for what seemed like ages. One of the bottles toppled from the shelf, and shattered into tiny pieces on the floor.

The children and their mother huddled together in the corner of the pharmacia, waiting for the earth tremors to pass.

Back at the governor's palace, Governor Grusius was sickened by the earthquake.

"What is going on?" he said shakily. "What is happening? I command the ground to stop moving!"

He hated this town already, with its boring fields of grapes and olives. And now, the ground beneath his feet shook every few minutes.

Grusius stared out one of the windows, and saw a tiny wisp of smoke swirling from the peak of Mount Pyros.

"It's my mountain grumbling," he said to himself, while reassuring himself that his palace was not about to shake itself to pieces. He had seen plenty of mountains, and felt the tremble of many earthquakes during his travels throughout the Roman empire. This was nothing to worry about. It would soon pass.

Governor Grusius's thoughts were soon interrupted by the sound of centurions' boots, marching rapidly towards his room. He sat down on his chair, and watched as the door was swung open.

"The man called Archius," announced a centurion. Archius was pushed roughly into the centre of the room, where he stood silently, being careful not to look directly at the governor.

"The famous Archius!" declared Grusius. "At last, we meet."

Archius bowed his head.

"They say you are the best medicine maker in the whole of the Roman empire," said Grusius. "From now on, you will work only for me," he ordered. "I have a special job for you."

Archius allowed himself a glance at the governor who was slouched on the chair. "Marina was right," he thought silently. "He is a bully. A lazy one at that."

"My uncle, the emperor, thinks he can do anything he wants," sneered Grusius. "But I know he is only a mere mortal, like his father, and his grandfather, and his great-grandfather. And, like all mere mortals, one day he will die."

The governor stood up, and waddled across the room to Archius.

"Some people think that because they do great things, their name will live forever. I, on the other hand, have a much better plan. My name, too, will be known hundreds of years from now — but it will not only be my name that lives forever." The governor squinted at Archius, the master medicine maker, with his beady eyes.

"You will make me a medicine — a potion — that will make me *live* forever," he said simply.

Archius couldn't help but stare at the governor. Not only was he a bully, he was mad, too!

"But ..." started Archius. The governor leaned closer and fixed him with a glare.

"No buts!" he barked. "You will find a way to make a potion that makes people immortal, that will make *me* immortal! If you cannot, you will find out how mortal you are yourself. Very quickly!"

"I have heard of people trying to make these medicines before," replied Archius. "But the ingredients are enormously expensive. You need herbs from the unexplored lands to the east, extracts from the hot desert lands to the south and iced water from the frozen lands to the north."

"I don't care how expensive it is," replied the governor sullenly. "Money is no problem. Just make me my potion."

Archius bowed again, and walked backwards out of the room. His head was spinning. How was he going to make this medicine? Where was he going to find the herbs, extracts and water he needed? How would the governor pay for the precious ingredients?

Again, without warning, the ground beneath his feet shook, and another threatening rumble bellowed from Mount Pyros. A thin line of smoke wove its way slowly skyward into the unknown.

"These are dangerous times," thought Archius, as he quickly made his way home.

Very dangerous times.

Chapter 3

Dangerous Times

True to his word, money was no problem for the governor. Grusius simply increased all the taxes immediately. The townspeople were charged taxes for bread, taxes for water, taxes for horses and cattle, and taxes for the number of children in their family.

The centurions collected the taxes each week, marching from house to house, banging on doors, stuffing the coins they gathered into huge sacks and leaving the people to starve.

Poor Archius was forced to work day and night,
gathering ancient recipes, manuscripts and scrolls.
He studied long after the moon had risen, writing
lists of ingredients to send to the governor.

Within days, strange pots and sacks and glass jars, bearing inscriptions in foreign languages, were delivered to the pharmacia. From dawn until dusk Archius mixed and ground and boiled the ingredients. "How I miss being with my wife and children," he would sigh.

Mount Pyros grumbled and groaned, the earth shook, and the smoke from the peak began to hang like a thick, bitter cloud over the town of Polonium. People came to the pharmacia, complaining of sore throats and headaches but, sadly, Archius had no choice other than to turn them away.

"I can only work for Governor Grusius," Archius explained helplessly. "I must obey his command."

The townspeople grew scared and began to believe they were cursed. The governor had brought nothing but bad luck and heavy taxes to their town. Even the mountain was angry!

Still, everyone was even more terrified of the fierce centurions, and no-one dared to complain.

Inside his palace, the governor began planning for his immortality. He ordered the name 'GRUSIUS' to be carved in huge letters above the entrance to his chambers.

He used the extra money he had demanded in taxes to buy the finest furniture and sent merchants to every corner of the empire to satisfy his greed. "If I am to live forever, it shall be in the best of luxury," he commanded.

The finest silks were brought from the east and the smoothest marble was brought from the quarries in the north. The palace sculptors were told to carve statues, all to look like Grusius.

Every day, he sent centurions to the pharmacia, to check on Archius's progress. Like the towering mountain overlooking the town, Grusius was becoming impatient, and his temper was becoming more fiery.

Finally, after months of research Archius believed he had uncovered the secret to immortality. His potion was almost ready.

Young Antonius crept into the pharmacia, and watched his father leaning over his desk.

"Will it work?" he asked.

Archius turned around, and Antonius was startled by his father's appearance. He looked thin and tired, and his eyes looked worried. His grey hair was frazzled, and his hands were stained black from the strange chemicals and herbs he had been using.

Archius smiled at his son, trying to disguise the sadness and the anxiety he felt.

"If it does, how would we know?" he replied. "Grusius won't let *us* try it. I suspect we will never find out if he lives forever."

The ground beneath their feet shook again.
The tremors were becoming worse and worse,
and more frequent.

"Where is your sister, Marina?" asked Archius.
Antonius shrugged.

"She's playing marbles again. I don't know why
she bothers. Every time she arranges them in the
circle, the ground shakes them all over the place."

Archius picked up a tiny glass jar, and stared at it. With a final shake of his head, he inserted a cork, took a deep breath, and turned to Antonius.

"Go and find Marina, and tell your mother to get things ready. My work is finished, and our time is short. You must all be ready to leave the *instant* that I return."

Antonius didn't argue. He didn't know where his father wanted them to go or what his mother would be getting things ready for — but he could tell that his father was worried. Perhaps it was the dangerous mountain; or perhaps it was the even more dangerous Grusius. Both were unpredictable.

Two centurions were standing guard outside Archius's doorway. They followed closely behind as he walked swiftly to the palace. Swords drawn, they glared furiously at any other person who dared to come close.

"Archius, we need medicine," called people from windows and doorways.

But the centurions would not let Archius answer. He struggled to keep walking through the black cloud, which blew down from the sizzling mountain.

His throat burned when he breathed in and even though it was only midday, the smoke prevented the sun's light from reaching the town. It seemed like dusk. And all the time, the ground lurched and swayed beneath him.

"Not a moment too soon!" bellowed Grusius, when Archius was finally ushered into the governor's room. "I hope you have used my money well! You certainly spent enough of it!"

Archius nodded, and withdrew the glass jar from his robe.

"It is finished, governor," he said.

"And *no-one* else knows the recipe?" asked Grusius, eyeing Archius suspiciously. He snatched the jar rudely from Archius's hand, and peered greedily at the dark liquid inside.

"No-one," replied Archius.

"Good," said Grusius. "Then your work is finished. And so are you! Centurions!"

A group of centurions drew their swords,
and walked threateningly towards Archius.

"But ... but ...," he cried.

Grusius sneered at the master medicine maker.

"You didn't think I'd let you live?" he asked.
"So you could give your recipe to others? Grusius,
and Grusius alone, shall become immortal!"

Suddenly, a thunderous roar burst forth from
outside the room. The floor swayed like a giant
wave, and the centurions staggered to keep their
balance. Archius seized his chance, and leapt
towards the door.

A mighty swoosh sliced the air as the blade of
a sword just missed Archius's head. He ran,
stumbling out the doorway and onto the steps.
Another tremendous boom split the dark air

around Polonium, and the seven columns of the governor's palace swayed dangerously. Pieces of stone crumbled and clattered to the ground.

Archius tore through the streets, leaving the centurions far behind. All around him, the town was in panic. High behind Polonium, at the peak of Mount Pyros, a terrifying red glow had appeared. Archius knew he didn't have a second to spare. If the centurions didn't get him, the mountain would.

Archius raced towards the pharmacia. He tumbled to his knees as another gigantic shake swept the ground from underneath him.

"Antonius! Marina!" he called desperately. "Where are you? Where is your mother?"

From out of the running crowds, Archius suddenly recognised three faces and breathed a sigh of relief.

"Marina wouldn't stop playing marbles!" accused
Antonius furiously. "We had to find her and drag
her away!"

"Quickly!" shouted Archius. "Gather your things.
We must escape immediately!"

Moments later, loaded down by their most valuable possessions, the family ran for their lives.

Behind them, a terrible sight emerged from the smoke and ash that blotted out the sun. A rolling, twisting mass of mud, ash and lava was tumbling down the mountainside at a terrifying speed.

＊ ＊ ＊ ＊ ＊

Inside the palace, Grusius had ordered all of his centurions to leave him alone. He stood trembling in his room, eyeing the glass jar he held in his shaking hands. A gigantic crack appeared in the mosaic tiled floor, but Grusius just grinned.

"With this potion I am immortal. Nothing can kill me," he said, foolishly.

Outside, a rolling, roaring noise that sounded like thunder grew and grew until it was deafening.

Suddenly, the room became darker than night, as the mud and ash racing down the mountain hit the first of the houses in Polonium, burying them instantly in molten rock.

Grusius laughed crazily.

"Immortality!" he cried, uncorking the jar. With one long swig, he drained the contents.

Just like a tornado, a terrific gust of wind sucked all the air out of the room, while a split second later, an enormous explosion of ash, smoke and mud tore through the whole palace.

For an instant, there was no noise, except for the smash of an empty glass jar on the stone floor.

Then the mountain erupted into its full fury, spewing smoke and thousands of tonnes of mud and ash over what was once the town of Polonium. The last sound to be heard from the palace was a faint cry, muffled by metres of ash and mud.

"Help! Get me out of here!"

Within minutes, the town was no more. And there was complete silence. A long, dark, undisturbed silence that lasted for thousands of years.

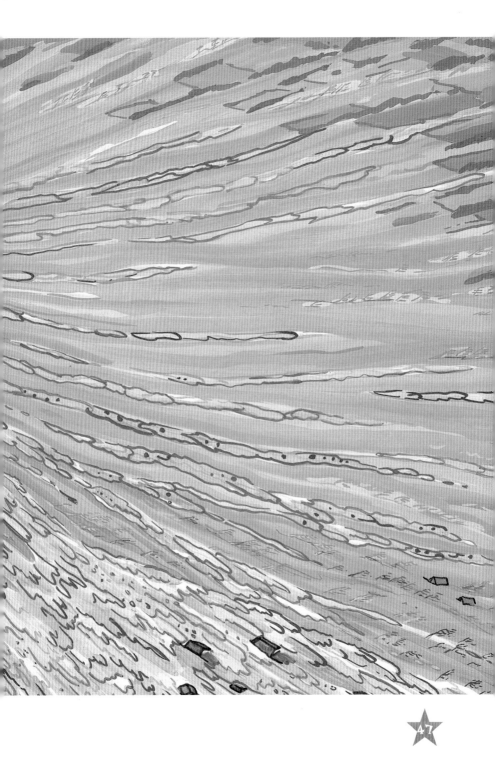